the good little girl

A Picture Yearling Book

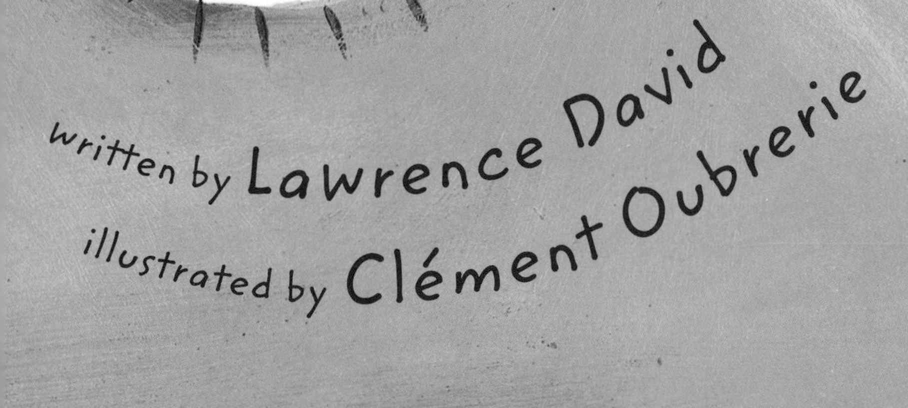

for Madeline David and Christopher David

L.E.D.

To all my friends who live in fabulous New York City

C.O.

Published by
Picture Yearling
an imprint of
Random House Children's Books
a division of Random House, Inc.
1540 Broadway
New York, New York 10036

ISBN: 0-440-41520-9
Reprinted by arrangement with Doubleday Books for Young Readers
Printed in the United States of America
May 2000
10 9 8 7 6 5 4 3 2 1

Miranda sat on the living room couch with her storybook closed in her lap. She looked out the window at the empty driveway. Friday night dinnertime and still no Mom or Dad home from work. Miranda's stomach rumbled, tickling her insides.

"Are you sure you don't want something to eat now?" Miranda's sitter asked.

"Oh, no," Miranda answered. "I want to eat with Mom and Dad. I can wait."

The sitter looked at her watch.

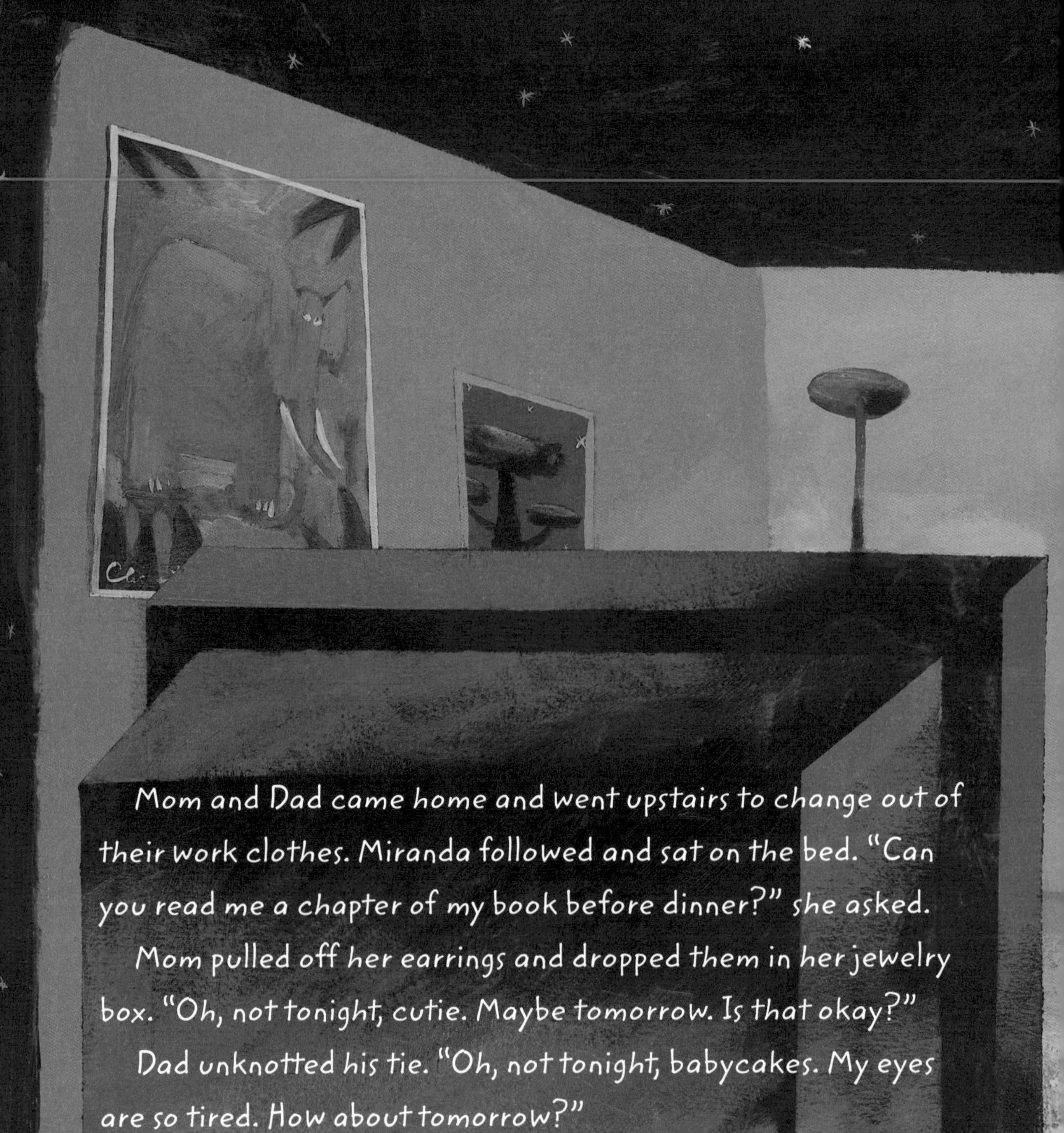

Mom and Dad came home and went upstairs to change out of their work clothes. Miranda followed and sat on the bed. "Can you read me a chapter of my book before dinner?" she asked.

Mom pulled off her earrings and dropped them in her jewelry box. "Oh, not tonight, cutie. Maybe tomorrow. Is that okay?"

Dad unknotted his tie. "Oh, not tonight, babycakes. My eyes are so tired. How about tomorrow?"

"Sure. Tomorrow's okay," Miranda replied.

After dinner, Miranda, Dad, and Mom settled on the couch and watched a movie on TV. Miranda smiled at her mom. "Do you like this show? I do."

Mom's eyes were closed and her mouth hung open.

Miranda laughed. "Dad, look how funny Mom is."

Dad said nothing. His eyes were closed too. He let out a growly snore.

Miranda shut off the TV. "That's okay," she told her dozing parents, "I can tuck myself in. We'll spend time together tomorrow at Saturday Family Waffle Breakfast."

Miranda loved Saturday Family Waffle Breakfast. That was her favorite time of the week.

Miranda woke Saturday morning to find a sunny spring day outside her window. Tomorrow had come, and it would be a good day because it was Saturday Family Waffle Breakfast.

"Hello, honey," said Mom. She stood at the stove waving a spatula. "Have a seat. Breakfast's almost ready."

"Hello, sweetie," said Dad. He sat at the table reading a book.

Miranda sat next to him. "What are you reading?"

Her dad turned a page. Her mom set a plate in front of Miranda.

Miranda gasped. Two gooshy, slimy egg eyes stared up at her. How rude of those eggs to stare! Beneath them were two squiggly, mean lips of bacon. How rude of the bacon to make such a mean face!

"Excuse me, Mom, but Saturday is Family Waffle Breakfast, remember?" Miranda reminded her mom.

Mom sat at the table. "We were all out of the mix, honey, and I forgot to pick up more. We'll have them tomorrow. That's okay, isn't it?"

The ugly egg eyes and squiggly bacon mouth laughed at Miranda. "That's okay," she said cheerfully, but something in her head felt different, someone inside her felt that eggs on Saturday Family Waffle Breakfast day was very, very, very *not* okay.

She remembered feeling
like this just last week at recess
when Rhoda Tashiagloo cut in front of her
at the water fountain.

But Miranda hadn't done
anything about it.

This time, Miranda could feel her body shaking, and then, right before her eyes,

her skin changed color from a pinkish white to an ugly green.

Her fingernails turned black and curly.

Her hair twisted into knots,

her lips snarled,

and her eyes turned from brown to red.

Miranda felt herself shrinking,

growing smaller

and smaller

and smaller

until she was just

a tiny little girl

inside the head

of this mean

green

girl.

Miranda stood behind the

girl's eyes. When she

looked out, she could

see her mom and dad.

"What's happening?" she called.

"*They can't hear you,*" the green girl said to Miranda from inside her head. "*They can only hear me when I talk.*"

"*Who are you?*" Miranda asked. "*Have I met you before?*"

"*I'm Lucretia,*" the girl replied. "*I wanted to come out and help when Rhoda Tashiagloo pushed in front of you at the water fountain, but you wouldn't let me.*"

"*Why are you here now?*" Miranda asked.

"*Aren't you hungry for waffles?*" Lucretia asked.

Miranda smiled, remembering. "*Oh, yes, very, very.*"

"Then sit back and watch," Lucretia instructed.

Lucretia sat up in the chair. "Hey!" she yelled at Miranda's mom and dad. "I don't want this yucky eggs and bacon! I want waffles and I want them now!"

Mom and Dad looked up from their food.

"Who are you?" Dad asked.

"Where's Miranda?" Mom asked.

"Miranda went away," Lucretia replied. "And she won't be coming back unless you give us waffles now."

"Then she'll come back?" Dad asked.

"Then our good little girl will return?" Mom asked.

"We'll see," Lucretia answered.

Mom, Dad, and Lucretia sat in Wally's Waffle Hut. Lucretia ate a huge waffle smothered with whipped cream, blueberries, and vanilla ice cream. Miranda sat in Lucretia's head and could taste the waffles filling Lucretia's stomach.

"Delicious," Miranda said. *"Thank you so much, Lucretia. You're a good friend to have."*

"We fed you waffles," Mom said to Lucretia. "Can Miranda come back now?"

"*What do you think?*" Lucretia asked Miranda. "*Do you want to come back yet? Or is there something else I can get you?*"

"*Hmmm . . . ,*" thought Miranda. She put a finger to her lips. "*Hmmm . . .*"

Fifteen minutes later, Mom, Dad, and Lucretia were at Kiddyland. They spent the afternoon doing all the things Miranda told Lucretia she loved the most. They ate cotton candy, played the ring toss game, and rode the merry-go-round, the Mother Goose Train, and the Spaceship to Mars.

On the Loop-the-Loop, Miranda was tossed around inside Lucretia's head so much she nearly got sick. *"I've had enough of Kiddyland,"* Miranda told her new friend. *"I think it's time to go home."*

"Don't you want more?" Lucretia asked. *"I can get you whatever you want."*

"Hmmm . . ." Miranda thought for a moment. *"How about if on the ride home, I sit in the front seat and play the radio?"*

"That's all?" Lucretia asked. *"Wouldn't you rather go on a balloon ride to the moon or get a new dress with a big red bow? That's what I'd like."*

"Well, all I'd like is to go home and play the radio in the car," Miranda said.

Lucretia pouted. *"You're not a very fun friend."*

"Sorry," Miranda said.

Lucretia told Mom and Dad what Miranda wanted.

"If we let you play the radio, will Miranda come back?" Mom asked sadly.

"We'll see," Lucretia said.

"Hmmm . . . ," Miranda thought. *"How do I come back, Lucretia? You never told me."*

"When you're ready, then you'll come back," Lucretia answered.

"I don't understand," Miranda said. *"When will I be ready?"*

"I don't know," Lucretia said. *"Maybe soon. Maybe never."*

All the way home, Lucretia pushed the radio buttons and played the songs as loudly as the radio could go. Mom covered her ears. Dad frowned. *"Maybe we should turn it down,"* Miranda said to Lucretia.

"I don't think so," Lucretia told Miranda.

Miranda buried her head in her arms. *"When we get home, I'm going to come back."*

"We'll see," Lucretia answered.

As they drove through town, Lucretia spotted Madeline's Beauty Salon. "Stop," she shouted.

Dad slammed on the brakes. Miranda fell against the inside of Lucretia's head.

Lucretia pointed at the beauty salon. "I want Mom to have her hair curled and dyed blue. I want Dad to have all his hair cut off."

Miranda's parents looked at each other.

"What if we don't?" Mom asked.

"What happens then?" Dad asked.

"I don't think that's nice," Miranda said to Lucretia.

Lucretia ignored Miranda. She laughed loudly. "If you don't do it, Miranda will never come back," she told them.

Miranda watched as her mom and dad got out of the car and walked into the beauty parlor.

"I don't think this is fun," Miranda said.

"Who asked you?" Lucretia replied. *"I'm the one in charge. I'm the one who got you the waffles. I'm the one who got you to Kiddyland. What do you ever get? 'Tomorrow.' 'Tomorrow' is all you get. I get it now, when you want it."*

"I don't like you anymore," Miranda told Lucretia.

"I don't care," Lucretia answered.

Fifteen minutes later, Miranda saw her mom and dad come out of the beauty salon. Mom's hair was blue and very curly. Dad's head had no hair on it at all.

"Can Miranda come back now?" Mom asked.

"Later," Lucretia replied.

Miranda shook her head and wiped her tears away. "*Sorry, Mom,*" she said. "*Sorry, Dad.*"

"*Hush up, baby,*" Lucretia told her.

Back home, Lucretia told Mom and Dad to sit down and listen to the list of things she wanted them to do.

"I want to come back now," Miranda told Lucretia. *"Tell me how to come back."*

"When you're ready, you'll come back," Lucretia told her. *"Now leave me alone. I'm busy."*

Lucretia stood in front of Miranda's parents and pointed with a finger. "Dad, if you want your good little girl back, you have to

...put on a dress and dance the Watusi.

Mom, you have to clean the chimney with your tongue.

Dad, you have to eat a bowl of spaghetti with peanut butter and meatball sauce.

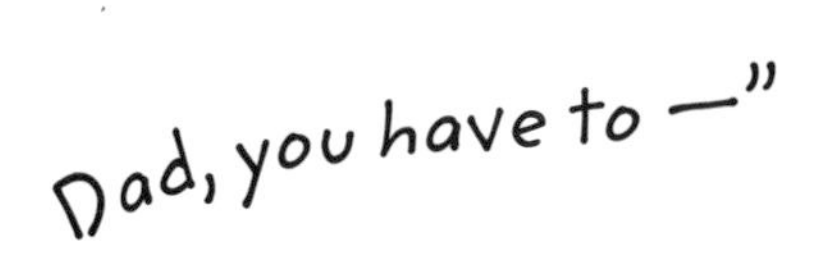

Mom, you have to stick pencils up your nose and sing 'Polly Wolly Doodle.'

Dad, you have to —"

"NOOOOO!" Miranda yelled at the top of her voice. "*LEAVE MY MOM AND DAD ALONE!*" She stood and reached out, poking Lucretia in one of her eyes.

"*Youch!*" Lucretia yelped. "*What do you want?*"

"*I HATE YOU!*" Miranda screamed. "*YOU'RE ONLY MEAN. NEVER NICE!*"

Miranda stomped around inside Lucretia's head, getting

angrier

and

angrier.

She felt her arms begin to grow. She felt her legs begin to grow. She was ready to come back and she was ready to come back now!

She pounded her feet harder.

"*No! Stop!*" Lucretia yelled.

Lucretia's skin changed from an ugly green to a pinkish white.

Her hair changed from being all knots to being straight and untangled.

Her eyes changed color from red to brown.

Her mouth stopped snarling and her long black fingernails became short and pink.

As Miranda grew and came back, Lucretia shrank and shrank until she was just a little mean, green girl inside Miranda's head.

Miranda had returned to herself.

Mom and Dad rushed to their little girl. They each gave Miranda a hug and a kiss.

"I'm sorry I let her turn up the radio and make you change your hair," Miranda told her parents.

"We're just glad she's gone," Dad said.

"We certainly are," Mom said. "It's awful having such a bossy, tough child when we're used to having such a good little girl."

Miranda put her hands on her hips. "Sometimes a good little girl might have to be a little bossy and tough," she said. "Or she might not get what she really needs."

"Has that happened to you?" Mom asked.

"Only sometimes," Miranda said.

"Well, we're sorry about that," Dad said.

"We'll try to remember better in the future, okay?" Mom said.

Miranda smiled. "Okay."

Mom looked at her watch. "Well, I'd better go take my bath now before dinner."

Dad looked at his watch. "And I really do want to watch that ball game on TV."

They both began to walk out of the room.

"Wait!" Miranda called.
Her parents stopped.
"Wait for what?" Mom asked.
"Is something wrong?" Dad asked.

Miranda looked down at her feet. She kicked the carpet. She spoke quietly. "I want you both to read me a story."

"When?" Mom asked. "Tomorrow?"

"Is tomorrow okay?" Dad asked.

"NOW!" Lucretia yelled inside Miranda's head. *"Ask for it NOW!"* "Hmmm . . ." Miranda thought for a moment. Tomorrow was too far away for her to wait. If she chose now, her parents couldn't do what they wanted to do.

"How about in one hour?" Miranda asked. "Is one hour okay?" Mom laughed. "That's perfectly okay, sweetie." Dad grinned. "We'd love to, honey. I'm glad you could ask."

One hour later, Mom, Dad, and Miranda sat on the porch swing. Mom and Dad read Miranda a story, taking turns with the voices. Lucretia sat up inside Miranda's head. She peered out through Miranda's eyes to see the pictures in the book.

Both Miranda and Lucretia had
big smiles on their faces.